Geronimo Stilton
ENGLISH!

12 MY FAMILY 我的家人

新雅文化事業有限公司
www.sunya.com.hk

Geronimo Stilton English
MY FAMILY　我的家人

作　　者：Geronimo Stilton 謝利連摩·史提頓
譯　　者：申倩
責任編輯：王燕參
封面繪圖：Giuseppe Facciotto
插圖繪畫：Claudio Cernuschi, Andrea Denegri, Daria Cerchi
內文設計：Angela Ficarelli, Raffaella Picozzi
出　　版：新雅文化事業有限公司
　　　　　香港筲箕灣耀興道3號東匯廣場9樓
　　　　　營銷部電話：（852）2562 0161
　　　　　客戶服務部電話：（852）2976 6559
　　　　　傳真：（852）2597 4003
　　　　　網址：http://www.sunya.com.hk
　　　　　電郵：marketing@sunya.com.hk
發　　行：香港聯合書刊物流有限公司
　　　　　香港新界大埔汀麗路36號中華商務印刷大廈3字樓
　　　　　電話：（852）2150 2100　傳真：（852）2407 3062
　　　　　電郵：info@suplogistics.com.hk
印　　刷：C & C Offset Printing Co.,Ltd
　　　　　香港新界大埔汀麗路36號
版　　次：二〇一一年六月初版
　　　　　10 9 8 7 6 5 4 3 2 1

ISBN: 978-962-08-5368-5
© 2007 Edizioni Piemme S.p.A., Via Tiziano 32 - 20145 Milano - Italia
International Rights © 2007 Atlantyca S.p.A. - via Leopardi, 8, Milano - Italy
© 2011 for this Work in Traditional Chinese language, Sun Ya Publications (HK) Ltd.
9/F, Eastern Central Plaza, 3 Yiu Hing Rd, Shau Kei Wan, Hong Kong
Published and printed in Hong Kong

老鼠記者精英會 ★ 會

Geronimo Stilton English Club

成為會員，可參加英語培訓課程，以及暢遊世界各地學英語，包括香港、歐洲、美加等。

參加表格

同時成為新雅書迷會會員，更可享以下優惠包括：

★ 到指定門市及書展可獲購書優惠　　★ 最新優惠及活動資訊

★ 收到會訊《新雅家庭》　　　　　　★ 參加有趣益智的書迷會活動

填妥此表格傳真或郵寄至新雅文化事業有限公司市場部 (傳真號碼及地址載於背頁)

☐ 本人已是新雅書迷會會員 (編號：SY＿＿＿＿＿＿＿＿＿＿＿)

☐ 本人現想申請成為老鼠記者精英會及新雅書迷會會員。

姓名 ＿＿＿＿＿＿＿＿＿＿＿＿＿＿＿＿＿＿　性別：＿＿＿＿＿

出生日期：＿＿＿＿＿ 年 ＿＿＿＿ 月 ＿＿＿ 日　年齡：＿＿＿＿＿

日間聯絡電話：＿＿＿＿＿＿＿＿＿＿＿＿＿＿＿＿＿＿＿＿＿＿＿＿＿

學校：＿＿＿＿＿＿＿＿＿＿＿＿＿＿＿＿＿＿＿＿＿＿＿＿＿＿＿＿＿

電郵：＿＿＿＿＿＿＿＿＿＿＿＿＿＿＿＿＿＿＿＿＿＿＿＿＿＿＿＿＿

職業：☐ 學生　☐ 家長　☐ 教師　☐ 其他 ＿＿＿＿＿＿＿＿＿＿＿

教育程度：☐ 小學以下　☐ 小學 (＿＿＿ 年級) ☐ 中學 (F.＿＿＿)

　　　　　☐ 大專　☐ 其他 ＿＿＿＿＿＿＿＿＿＿＿＿＿＿＿＿＿＿

從哪本書獲得此表格：＿＿＿＿＿＿＿＿＿＿＿＿＿＿＿＿＿＿＿＿＿＿

地址 (必須以**英文**填寫)：＿＿＿＿＿＿Room(室)＿＿＿＿＿Floor(樓)

＿＿＿＿＿＿Block(座)＿＿＿＿＿＿＿＿＿＿＿＿Building(大廈)

＿＿＿＿＿＿＿＿＿＿＿＿＿＿＿＿＿＿＿＿＿＿Eastate (屋邨 / 屋苑)

＿＿＿＿＿＿Street No.(街號)＿＿＿＿＿＿＿＿＿＿Street(街道)

＿＿＿＿＿＿District(區域)HK/KLN/NT＊(＊請刪去不適用者)

以上會員資料只作為本公司記錄、推廣及聯絡之用途，一切絕對保密。

新雅文化事業有限公司

老鼠記者精英會
Geronimo Stilton English Club

香港筲箕灣耀興道 3 號
東匯廣場 9 樓

新雅文化事業有限公司

CONTENTS
目錄

BENJAMIN'S CLASSMATES
班哲文的老師和同學們

Maestra Topitilla
托比蒂拉・德・托比莉斯

Rarin
拉琳

Diego
迪哥

Rupa
露芭

Tui
杜爾

David
大衛

Sakura
櫻花

Mohamed
穆哈麥德

Tian Kai
田凱

Oliver
奧利佛

Milenko
米蘭哥

Trippo
特里普

Carmen
卡敏

Atina
阿提娜

Esmeralda
愛絲梅拉達

Pandora
潘朵拉

Takeshi
北野

Kuti
菊花

Benjamin
班哲文

Hsing
阿星

Laura
羅拉

Kiku
奇哥

Antonia
安東妮婭

Liza
麗莎

GERONIMO AND HIS FRIENDS
謝利連摩和他的家鼠朋友們

謝利連摩・史提頓 Geronimo Stilton

一個古怪的傢伙，簡直可以說是一隻笨拙的文化鼠。他是《鼠民公報》的總裁，正花盡心思改變報紙業的歷史。

菲・史提頓 Tea Stilton

謝利連摩的妹妹，她是《鼠民公報》的特派記者，同時也是一個運動愛好者。

班哲文・史提頓 Benjamin Stilton

謝利連摩的小侄兒，常被叔叔稱作「我的小乳酪」，是一隻感情豐富的小老鼠。

潘朵拉・華之鼠 Pandora Woz

柏蒂・活力鼠的姨甥女、班哲文最好的朋友，是一隻活潑開朗的小老鼠。

柏蒂・活力鼠 Patty Spring

美麗迷人的電視新聞工作者，致力於她熱愛的電視事業。

賴皮 Trappola

謝利連摩的表弟，非常喜歡食物，風趣幽默，是一隻饞嘴、愛開玩笑的老鼠，善於將歡樂傳遞給每一隻鼠。

麗萍姑媽 Zia Lippa

謝利連摩的姑媽，對鼠十分友善，又和藹可親，只想將最好的給身邊的鼠。

艾拿 Iena

謝利連摩的好朋友，充滿活力，熱愛各項運動，他希望能把對運動的熱誠傳給謝利連摩。

史奎克・愛管閒事鼠 Ficcanaso Squitt

謝利連摩的好朋友，是一個非常有頭腦的私家偵探，總是穿着一件黃色的乾濕褸。

THIS IS MY FAMILY!
這是我的家人！

親愛的小朋友，我們又見面了！你想不想認識我的……呃……「女朋友」——其實也差不多是「未婚妻」了——柏蒂・活力鼠的家人呢？柏蒂的家人可多了，而且每一個都很友善！我以一千塊莫澤雷勒乳酪發誓，這真是個學習用英語稱呼家人的最好機會。我現在就要和柏蒂一起出發去她的家了，可是班哲文和潘朵拉不能跟着一起去，因為今天他們都要去上學。

We'll be back soon.

Goodbye!

跟我謝利連摩·史提頓一起學英文，就像玩遊戲一樣簡單好玩！

你可以一邊看着圖畫一邊讀。以下有幾個標誌，你要特別留意：

當看到 ⓒ 標誌時，你可以聽CD，一邊聽，一邊跟着朗讀，還可以跟着一起唱歌。

當看到 ★ 標誌時，你可以和朋友們一起玩遊戲，或者嘗試回答問題。題目很簡單，它們對鞏固你所學過的內容很有幫助。

當看到 ❗ 標誌時，你要注意看一下格子裏的生字，反覆唸幾遍，掌握發音。

最後，不要忘記完成小測驗和練習冊裏的問題！看看你有多聰明吧。

祝大家學得開開心心！

謝利連摩·史提頓

HOW DO YOU DO? 你好嗎？

活力鼠一家住在巨杉山谷一幢漂亮的房子裏。當我和柏蒂到達的時候，活力鼠一家連忙出來歡迎我們。大家都迫不及待地想看看柏蒂的男朋友，那當然是我啦！柏蒂向我介紹她的家人，你也跟着一起說說看。

Geronimo, let me introduce you to my grandfather and grandmother.

Pleased to meet you!

Geronimo, this is my father, Bobby Spring.

Hello!

And this is my mother, Susy Rattella.

Pleased to meet you!

This is Dakota, my twin brother.

Hello!

And this is my sister, Armadilla.

How do you do?

This is my uncle, Teddy Spring.

Hello!

How Do You Do?

We are a happy family!
This is my father,
this is my mother,
this is my sister
and this is my brother,
in the evening
we sing together!

Mother always says
when you meet somebody
always greet him
how do you do?
Pleased to meet you!
And sing with us!

We are a happy family!
This is my uncle,
this is my aunt,
this is my nephew
and this is my niece,
in the evening
we sing together!

Mother always says
when you meet somebody
always greet him
how do you do?
Pleased to meet you!
And sing with us!

And this is my aunt, Jenny Zampina.

How do you do?

★ 1. 當別人向你介紹另一個人時，你可以說「你好嗎？」作回應，換成英語該怎麼説？

★ 2. 試用英語説出：「很高興認識你！」

答案：
1. How do you do?
2. Pleased to meet you!

9

THE SPRING FAMILY
活力鼠一家

我非常不好意思，我記不住柏蒂家人的名字，因為她的家人實在太多了。為了幫助我對她的家人有更深的印象，柏蒂一邊給我看她家人的照片，一邊給我逐一介紹有關他們的事情。你也跟着一起說說看。

Grandpa Spring is Patty Spring's grandfather. He's a nature scientist.

Grandma Spring is Patty Spring's grandmother. She travelled around the world when aeroplanes didn't exist yet.

Susy Rattella is Bobby Spring's wife and Patty Spring's mother.
She's fond of dolphins. She works for the Marine Centre in Topazia.

Bobby Spring is Grandpa and Grandma Spring's son, Susy Rattella's husband, Patty Spring's father.
He runs Spring Farm, a model farm.

This is me, Patty Spring! I'm Dakota's twin sister.

Dakota Spring is Susy Rattella and Bobby Spring's son, Patty Spring's twin brother.
He is a TV film director and travels the world to save nature.

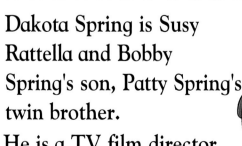

John Woz

Armadilla Spring

Ciccirillo

Pandora

Armadilla Spring is Susy Rattella and Bobby Spring's daughter. She is Patty Spring's sister. She married John Woz. They are Pandora and Ciccirillo's parents.

Teddy Spring is Grandpa and Grandma Spring's son, Patty Spring's uncle.

He runs Spring Farm together with his brother Bobby.

Jenny Zampina is Teddy Spring's wife and Patty Spring's aunt.

She's an excellent cook and the whole family loves her Yummy Cake.

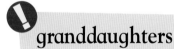

❗ granddaughters   孫女

Lolly

Lilly

Lally

Lily, Lally and Lolly Spring are Jenny Zampina and Teddy Spring's granddaughters.

11

PHOTOS　照片

時間過得很快，是時候回家了。我非常感謝柏蒂家人的熱情款待，我答應他們很快會再來探望他們。我以一千塊莫澤雷勒乳酪發誓，有個大家庭真好啊！

我回家後不久，班哲文和潘朵拉也放學回來了，我給他們講了白天去柏蒂家的事情，然後拿出自己家人的照片給他們看。班哲文和潘朵拉很快便學會了怎樣稱呼不同的家人，你也跟着一起說說看。

Geronimo is her brother.

She's my aunt. I'm her nephew.

This is Tea. She is Geronimo's sister.

This is Trappola. He is Geronimo's cousin.

Yes, he's my cousin.

He's your cousin.

This is Benjamin. He is Geronimo's nephew.

This is me! I'm Geronimo's nephew.

❗ nephew　侄子

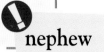

This is Grandpa Torquato.

He's Geronimo's grandfather.

This is Grandma Rosa.

She's your grandmother.

Yes, she's my grandmother.

This is Aunt Margarina and that is Uncle Mascarpone.

These are Aunt Lippa and Uncle Spelliccio.

They're my aunt and my uncle.

⭐ 你知道你爸爸媽媽的名字嗎？試着用英語給大家介紹你爸爸媽媽的名字吧。

This is ... He's my father.
This is ... She's my mother.

TALKING ABOUT...
講一些關於……

我每次看到自己親人的照
片時，心裏都會有很多感觸……
班哲文和潘朵拉也在看照片裏的
親人和朋友，他們不斷地談論着
各人的特徵，你也跟着一起說說
看。

Grandpa and
Grandma Spring
are quite old.

Tea Stilton is tall
and slim.

Aunt Lippa is
small and thin.

Dakota Spring is
tall and strong.

Lilly, Lally and
Lolly are young
and friendly.

Fontina and
Fonduta are
agile and slim.

Aunt Margarina is shorter than Uncle Mascarpone.

Uncle Spelliccio is taller than Aunt Lippa.

Lilly Spring is the youngest and the smallest of Jenny Zampina and Teddy Spring's granddaughters.

short   矮
shorter   比較矮
tall   高
taller   比較高
the smallest   最小的
the youngest   最年輕的

Who's taller? Me or her, Uncle Geronimo?

You are the same height.

TELL ME WHO THIS IS!
告訴我這是誰！

潘朵拉看着這些照片，突然想到一個好主意。她提議我們可以玩一個遊戲：我隨便抽出一張照片，然後由他們說出照片中的人是誰！

Who is this?

That's Tea Stilton.

Very good! She's my younger sister. She's a photographer. She isn't scared of anything.

Who is this?

That's Susy Rattella.

Very good! She knows everything about dolphins.

Who is this?

That's Patty Spring.

Very good! She's a TV journalist. She fights to defend the environment and to save animals.

Who is this?

That's Aunt Margarina.

Very good! She is Fontina and Fonduta's mother. Aunt Magarina always has a lovely smell of vanilla and freshly baked biscuits.

Who is this?

That's Armadilla Spring.

Very good! Who's her daughter?

I'm her daughter.

Who is this?

That's Trappola. He's your cousin.

Very good! And what does he do?

Well, he's always getting into trouble.

 試用英語說出：「這是誰啊？這是瑪嘉蓮姑媽。」

WHO AM I? 我是誰？

轉眼間，一個下午過去了，我覺得很開心，因為我擁有一個這麼美好的家庭。我突然想起來，史提頓家很久沒有舉行過家庭大聚會了！於是我馬上給所有親戚朋友打電話，請他們第二天來我家作客。果然第二天大家都來了。你認得他們嗎？請根據各鼠自己的介紹，用英語說出他們的名字吧！

I am fit and cheerful. Who am I? I am...

1

I am affectionate and patient. Who am I? I am...

I am Geronimo's grandfather. Who am I? I am...

2

3

I am greedy and messy. Who am I? I am...

I am lively and curious. Who am I? I am...

4

5

! niece 姨甥女

18

I am pleasant and sweet. Who am I? I am...

I am Geronimo's nephew. Who am I? I am...

I am Patty Spring's niece. Who am I? I am...

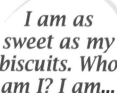

I am as sweet as my biscuits. Who am I? I am...

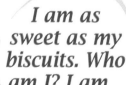

A SONG FOR YOU!

Track 2

My Family

Father, mother,
uncle, aunt,
sister, brother.
I love my family!

Grandfather and grandmother,
nephew, niece and cousin.

Grandfather and grandmother,
nephew, niece and cousin.

Oh oh oh oh
What a fantastic family!
This is my... family!
What a fantastic family!
This is my... family!

答案 :
1. Tea 2. Aunt Lippa 3. Torquato 4. Patty 5. Trappola
6. Geronimo 7. Benjamin 8. Pandora 9. Aunt Margarina

19

AN EXCITING DAY

Geronimo is staying with Patty Spring's parents, in the Giant Sequoia Valley.

〈令人興奮的一天〉

謝利連摩跟柏蒂‧活力鼠來到巨杉山谷探望她的爸爸媽媽，並且留下來跟他們小住數天。

柏蒂：為什麼我們不去硫磺湖遊覽一下？我們可以在那裏看到火山……

謝利連摩：當……當然好啦！

蘇絲：下午茶時間見！

柏蒂：謝利連摩，你準備好了嗎？
謝利連摩：當然準備好了！真高興能和你一起出去玩！

柏蒂小心地駕駛着，但是通往湖的那條路布滿了石頭，她的越野車顛簸得很厲害。

柏蒂：你怎樣了？　　　謝利連摩：我覺得……頭暈目眩。

柏蒂：看看四周美麗的風景吧！
謝利連摩：沒錯，風景是很美麗……但這些彎路很可怕！

謝利連摩：唉……我們快到達目的地了，是嗎？

柏蒂：你説得對，你怎麼知道的？

謝利連摩：(用力嗅了一下)……難道你聞不到那股臭味嗎？

柏蒂：臭味？我只聞到一股硫磺的氣味。

謝利連摩：……嗯，當然啦，我的意思是説我聞到一股……硫磺的氣味！

The bends slow them down and it gets late, too late to reach the lake...

然而，由於太多彎路令他們的車子慢了下來，所以他們來晚了，當他們到達湖的時候已經太晚了……

謝利連摩：你在做什麼？
柏蒂：我們來晚了！回家去吧！

柏蒂：下午茶時間快到了……我父母在等着我們呢……

謝利連摩：我有點暈車！我有一個建議……不如我走路回去！
柏蒂：但當你走路回到家時，可能只剩下蛋糕的碎屑！

The End

謝利連摩：想深一層後，我沒感到那麼不舒服了……好的，我們回家吧！

TEST 小測驗

⭐ 1. 用英語說出下面的人物稱謂。

(a) 叔叔　　(b) 爸爸　　(c) 爺爺

(d) 姑媽　　(e) 媽媽　　(f) 弟弟

(g) 外婆　　(h) 姐姐

⭐ 2. 讀出下面的句子，然後用中文說出它們的意思。

(a) These are my grandparents.　　(b) This is my mother.

(c) These are my parents.　　(d) This is my father.

⭐ 3. 用英語說出下面的句子。

(a) 柏蒂·活力鼠長得又高又苗條。

Patty Spring is ... and ...

(b) 達科他·活力鼠長得又高又強壯。

Dakota Spring is ... and ...

(c) 達科他·活力鼠比波比·活力鼠長得高。

Dakota Spring is ... than Bobby Spring.

(d) 莉莉·活力鼠比蘿莉·活力鼠長得矮。

Lilly Spring is ... than Lolly Spring.

Track 4

DICTIONARY 詞典

（英、粵、普發聲）

A

aeroplanes　飛機

affectionate　溫柔親切

agile　靈敏

animals　動物

anything　任何事情

aunt　伯母／嬸嬸／姑媽／
　　姨媽／舅母

awful　可怕

B

bends　彎路

biscuits　餅乾

brother　哥哥／弟弟

C

cake　蛋糕

carefully　小心地

carsick　暈車

centre　中心

cheerful　愉快的

children　小朋友

cook　廚師

cousin　表兄弟姊妹

crumbs　碎屑

curious　好奇的

D

daughter　女兒

defend　保護

dizzy　頭暈目眩

dolphins　海豚

drives　駕駛

E

environment　環境

excellent　出色的

exciting　令人興奮的

25

exist　存在

F

family　家人／家庭

farm　農場

father　爸爸

film director　導演

fond of　喜歡

friendly　友善

G

goodbye　再見

granddaughters　孫女

grandfather　爺爺／外公

grandmother

　嫲嫲（普：奶奶）／外婆

grandparents

　祖父母／外祖父母

greedy　貪吃

greet　打招呼

H

happy　開心的

height　高度

husband　丈夫

I

introduce　介紹

J

journalist　記者

K

know　知道

L

lake　湖

landscape　風景

lively　活潑的

look after　照顧

M

meet　認識

messy　混亂

mother　媽媽

N

nature　自然

nephew　侄子

nice　美好的

niece　姨甥女

O

of course　當然

off-road vehicle　越野車

on second thoughts

　　想深一層

P

parents　父母

patient　有耐性

photo　照片

photographer　攝影師

pleasant　和藹可親

pleased　高興

R

reach　到達

ready　準備好

right　對

runs　經營

S

save　拯救

scared　害怕

scent　氣味

scientist　科學家

short　矮

sing　唱歌

sister　姐姐 / 妹妹

slim　苗條

slow down　慢下來

smell　聞

son　兒子

soon　不久

stink　臭味

stones　石頭

strong　強壯

sulphur 硫磺

T

tall 高

thin 瘦

travels 旅行

trip 旅程

trouble 麻煩

twin 孿生的

U

uncle 伯父／叔叔／
　　姑丈／姨丈／舅父

V

vanilla 雲尼拿味
　　（普：香草味）

volcano 火山

W

walk 走路

whole 整個

wife 妻子

works 工作

world 世界

worry 擔心

Y

young 年輕

看在一千塊莫澤雷勒乳酪的份上，你學得開心嗎？很開心，對不對？好極了！跟你一起跳舞唱歌我也很開心！我等着你下次繼續跟班哲文和潘朵拉一起玩一起學英語呀。現在要說再見了，當然是用英語說啦！

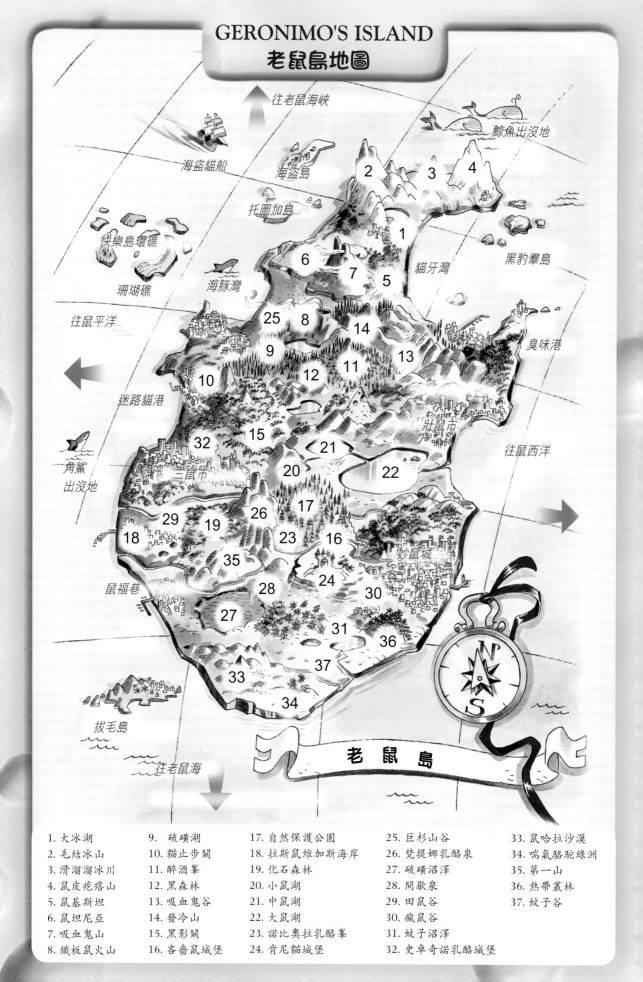

GERONIMO'S ISLAND
老鼠島地圖

往老鼠海峽

鯨魚出沒地

海盜貓船

海盜島

托圖加島

快樂島環礁

珊瑚礁

海豚灣

往鼠平洋

貓牙灣

黑豹羣島

臭味港

往鼠西洋

往鼠平洋

角鯊
出沒地

迷路貓港

壯鼠市

三鼠市

妙鼠城

鼠福巷

拔毛島

往老鼠海

老鼠島

1. 大冰湖	9. 硫磺湖	17. 自然保護公園	25. 巨杉山谷	33. 鼠哈拉沙漠
2. 毛結冰山	10. 貓止步關	18. 拉斯鼠維加斯海岸	26. 梵提娜乳酪泉	34. 喘氣駱駝綠洲
3. 滑溜溜冰川	11. 醉酒峯	19. 化石森林	27. 硫磺沼澤	35. 第一山
4. 鼠皮疙瘩山	12. 黑森林	20. 小鼠湖	28. 間歇泉	36. 熱帶叢林
5. 鼠基斯坦	13. 吸血鬼谷	21. 中鼠湖	29. 田鼠谷	37. 蚊子谷
6. 鼠坦尼亞	14. 發冷山	22. 大鼠湖	30. 瘋鼠谷	
7. 吸血鬼山	15. 黑影關	23. 諾比奧拉乳酪峯	31. 蚊子沼澤	
8. 鐵板鼠火山	16. 吝嗇鼠城堡	24. 肯尼貓城堡	32. 史卓奇諾乳酪城堡	

Geronimo Stilton

EXERCISE BOOK
練習冊

想知道自己對 MY FAMILY 掌握了多少，
趕快打開後面的練習完成它吧！

ENGLISH!

12 MY FAMILY 我的家人

MY FAMILY 我的家人

⭐ 依照不同的稱謂，在下面的相框中貼上你家人的照片，或者把他們的樣子畫出來，然後在橫線上寫出他們的名字。

My grandfather

_____

My grandmother

_____

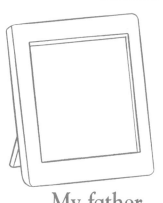

My father

_____

My mother

_____

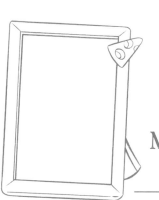

My brother

_____

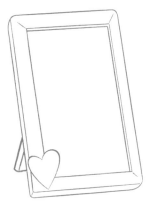

My sister

_____

GUESS WHO'S TALKING
猜猜誰在説話

⭐ 看看下面話框裏的句子，猜猜是誰在説話，參照例題，給每個話框加上小尾巴，小尾巴的方向要指着説話者。

例

I am Patty Spring's grandfather.

A. Grandpa Spring

B. Bobby Spring

1. *I am Patty Spring's grandmother.*

A. Grandma Spring

B. Jenny Zampina

2. *I am Patty Spring's mother.*

A. Grandma Spring

B. Susy Rattella

3.

I am Patty Spring's father.

A.

B.

Bobby
Spring

Grandpa
Spring

4.

I am Patty Spring's twin brother.

A.

B.

Dakota
Spring

Teddy
Spring

5.

I am Susy Rattella's daughter.

A.

B.

Patty
Spring

Dakota
Spring

6.

I am Patty Spring's aunt.

A.

B.

Armadilla
Spring

Jenny
Zampina

GUESS WHO SAYS THAT
猜猜是誰說的

⭐ 看看下面話框裏的句子，猜猜是誰說的，把話框與相應的說話者用線連起來。

1. Trappola

2. Tea

3. Benjamin

4. Pandora

A. *I am Benjamin's aunt.*

B. *I am Geronimo's little nephew.*

C. *I am Patty Spring's niece.*

D. *I am Geronimo's cousin.*

THREE LITTLE GIRLS
三個小女孩

⭐ 你認識柏蒂的三個侄女嗎？她們之中誰年紀最小？誰最高？從下面選出正確的詞彙填在橫線上，完成句子。

the youngest   taller   shorter   the smallest

1.

Lilly

Lilly Spring is _____

and _____ .

3.

Lally

2.

Lolly

Lally Spring is _____

than Lolly Spring.

Lolly Spring is _____

than Lilly and Lally Spring.

WHO ARE THEY?
他們是誰？

⭐ 看看下面的圖畫，你認識他們嗎？從下面選出正確的詞彙填在橫線上，完成句子。

animals   smell   dolphins   scared   biscuits
photographer   everything   journalist

1.

She is Patty Spring.

She is a TV _____ .

She fights to defend the environment

and to save _____ .

2.

She is Tea Stilton.

She is a

_____ . She

isn't _____

of anything.

Who are they?

3.

She is Aunt Margarina.

She always has a

lovely _____ of

vanilla and freshly baked

_____ .

4.

She is Susy Rattella.

She knows _____

about _____ .

ANSWERS 答案

TEST 小測驗

1. (a) uncle   (b) father   (c) grandfather   (d) aunt
    (e) mother   (f) brother   (g) grandmother   (h) sister

2. (a) 這是我的祖父母 / 外祖父母。
    (b) 這是我的媽媽。
    (c) 這是我的父母。
    (d) 這是我的爸爸。

3. (a) tall, slim   (b) tall, strong   (c) taller   (d) shorter

EXERCISE BOOK 練習冊

P.1
略

P.2-3
1. A   2. B   3. A   4. A   5. A   6. B

P.4
1. D   2. A   3. B   4. C

P.5
1. the youngest, the smallest   2. taller   3. shorter

P.6-7
1. journalist, animals
2. photographer, scared
3. smell, biscuits
4. everything, dolphins